THE POWER OF POETRY

Time To Have Our Say

Edited By Andrew Porter

First published in Great Britain in 2023 by:

 YoungWriters

Young Writers
Remus House
Coltsfoot Drive
Peterborough
PE2 9BF
Telephone: 01733 890066
Website: www.youngwriters.co.uk

All Rights Reserved
Book Design by Ashley Janson
© Copyright Contributors 2023
Softback ISBN 978-1-80459-618-0

Printed and bound in the UK by BookPrintingUK
Website: www.bookprintinguk.com
YB0546Y

FOREWORD

Since 1991, here at Young Writers we have celebrated the awesome power of creative writing, especially in young adults where it can serve as a vital method of expressing their emotions and views about the world around them. In every poem we see the effort and thought that each student published in this book has put into their work and by creating this anthology we hope to encourage them further with the ultimate goal of sparking a life-long love of writing.

Our latest competition for secondary school students, **The Power of Poetry,** challenged young writers to consider what was important to them and how to express that using the power of words. We wanted to give them a voice, the chance to express themselves freely and honestly, something which is so important for these young adults to feel confident and listened to. They could give an opinion, highlight an issue, consider a dilemma, impart advice or simply write about something they love. There were no restrictions on style or subject so you will find an anthology brimming with a variety of poetic styles and topics. We hope you find it as absorbing as we have.

We encourage young writers to express themselves and address subjects that matter to them, which sometimes means writing about sensitive or contentious topics. If you have been affected by any issues raised in this book, details on where to find help can be found at
www.youngwriters.co.uk/info/other/contact-lines

CONTENTS

ACS International School, Cobham

Imani Purnell (12)	1
Sanaya Sengupta (13)	2
Zahara Nisioti Spyropoulos (12)	4
Oskar Kjellberg (13)	6
Jiwoo Yang (15)	8
Julie Hammer (12)	11
Amalia Poyet (13)	12
Mia Blabolil (13)	14
Caitlin Phillips (13)	16
Cooper Bourgeois (12)	18
Ricardo Martinez (12)	19
Renee-Eleanore Schoors (12)	20
Matteo Emenalo (13)	21
Mia Crowther (13)	22
Jessica-Heather McDonald	23

Bourne Grammar School, Bourne

Emilia Beacham (16)	24

Bramhall High School, Bramhall

Amy Gardner (15)	26
Abbie Williams (13)	27
Olivia Cowan (12)	28
Elsie Gallo	30

Cokethorpe School, Witney

Grace Gunn (17)	32
Oscar Luckett	34
Florence Adepoju (17)	37
Dee Biles (17)	38
Serafina Conlon-Sangster (14)	40

Jordyn Everett (16)	41

Heckmondwike Grammar School, Heckmondwike

Anish Srikanth (16)	42

Hetton Academy, Houghton Le Spring

Chibueze Richard Ezebor (13)	43
Evan Lidster (16)	45

King Edward VI School, Lichfield

Isabelle Coleman (12)	47
Samantha Parkin (14)	48

Little Heath School, Tilehurst

Nico Girzynski (12)	50
Daisy Kinton (14)	52
Zimal Mansur	53
Laszlo Grant-Roberts (18)	54
Lara Hutt	55
Evelyn Card	56
Albert Maslewski	57

Merchants' Academy, Bristol

Madison Smith (12)	58
Klaus Isom (15)	60
Faith Smith Chivers (12)	62
Faith Pearce (13)	63
Jagoda Jastrzebska (13)	64
Jannat Khurram (17)	65

Northampton Academy, Northampton

Vendija Graudina (13)	66
Adam Sobocinski (12)	67
Natalia Stanciulescu (11)	68
Riyan Unadkat (12)	69
Tamara Floszmann (13)	70
Millie Laugharne (12)	71
Sophie Clarke (11)	72
Nikola Izosina (11)	73

Ormiston Rivers Academy, Burnham-On-Crouch

Eleanor Garlick (13)	74
Thomas Yates (13)	75

Pipers Corner School, Great Kingshill

Georgie Cordell (12)	76

Priory Academy, Dunstable

Dylan Marcelo (11)	77
Alice Bijum (14)	78
Armani Musamadya (13)	80
Ryan Brimmell (13)	82
Meghan Morris (11)	83
Lucas Bidaudville-Begley (12)	84

Ridgeway Academy, Welwyn Garden City

Kiara	85
Kaysie Davies (12)	86
Elizabeth Dawson (11)	88
Bella Flaherty (12)	90
Jonnell Mbangu	92
Harriet Jones (11)	93
George Rhodes	94
Chloe Thompson (12)	96
Eva Harrison (11)	98
Finn Stratton	99

Jojo Laci (15)	100
Lois Grostrate (11)	101
Dylan Bragg (12)	102
Amie Davies (12)	103
Ranulya Kotalawela (12)	104
Summer St John	105
Cassie Messer	106
Willow Beer (11)	107
Jayden Benford (11)	108
Rhys Stratton	109
Rafael Hilario (11)	110
Frank Rozanek (11)	111
Brandon Paterson (12)	112
Isabella Staines (11)	113
Lexi Gorman	114
Jayden Clarke	115
Cameron Burt (12)	116
Joshua Masson (12)	117
Eleanor McDonald (12)	118
Tom Rhodes	119
Lois Friend	120
Jake Vine (12)	121

Saltley School, Birmingham

Irum Ara (12)	122
Ayub Isxaaq	124
Samuel Abdin (12)	125

Sarah Bonnell School, Stratford

Emmeline Rhodes (11)	126
Lelas Elwan (12)	128
Saba Hoque (12)	129
Angela Tang (12)	130
Subaha Saif (13)	132
Fathia Mazumder (11)	134
Tasnim Mezhiche (11)	136
Rimzim Baser (14)	138
Zainab Chowdhury (11)	140
Naomi Chima (11)	141
Saimona Shamim (12)	142
Amanda Jakobsone (13)	143
Iram Mazumder (12)	144

Juri Bazan (12)	146
Liyana Begum (12)	147

St Joseph's College, Belfast

David Nugent (12)	148
Benny Weng (11)	150
Grace Duffin (13)	151
Mya McGrattan (14)	152
Zara Stalker (12)	153
Iona Hughes	154
Noel Kunnathparambil (14)	155
Arianna Marcos (13)	156
Innes White	157
Anna Mullan	158
Filip Niedziolka (13)	159
Aaron McKenna (12)	160
Tom Magee (14)	161
Lauren McCafferty (12)	162
Sarah Jane McCrumlish	163
Rachel Nelson	164

St Louis Grammar School, Kilkeel

Ciara Cunningham (12)	165
Jack Doran (11)	166
Miya Russell (11)	167
Emilia Rose Gren (12)	168

Stretford High School, Stretford

Jessica Housley (13)	169
Matthew Cooke (12)	170
Izah Maroof (13)	172
Inha Cho (13)	174
Khadijah Timol (12)	175
Eshal Nasir (13)	176
Stephanie Nyavi (12)	177
Eshal Chowdhary (13)	178
Kuljeet Singh (13)	179
Tayyaba Wahid (12)	180
Umaimah Bhana (12)	181
Marley Barrett (12)	182
Salman Alam (13)	183

Muhammed Ali (13)	184

Tarleton Academy, Tarleton

Isla Pullin	185
Joseph Vose (13)	186

THE POEMS

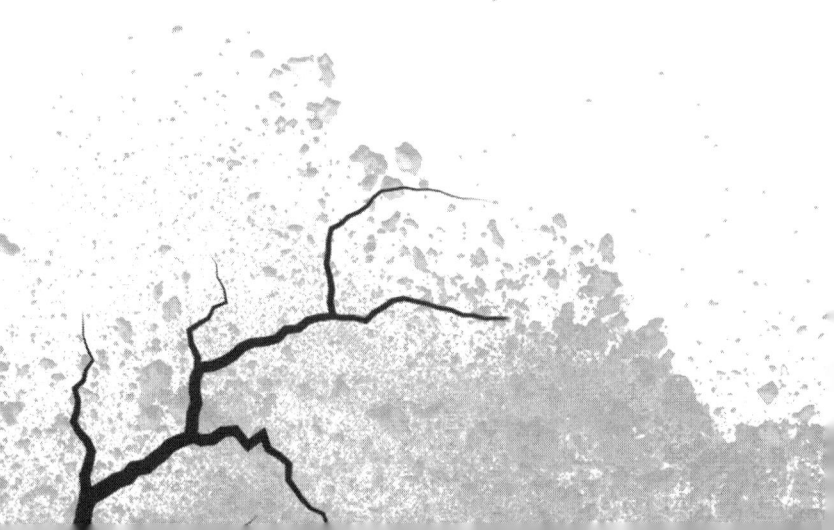

Imagine If Dreams Were Real...

If dreams were real your imagination could go wild.
Recapture the adventures that you had as a child.
You could be zooming in the blackness of outer space,
Or find yourself in any other place.
Sometimes you dream about sunshine that reaches
Into your darkest moments.
Sometimes you dream about blackness that freezes your heart.
If dreams were real you could make up anything you wanted.
You could be a horse
Galloping free as the wind.
You could use the Force
To be the best version of yourself.

What happens in a nightmare?
You won't be able to feel the fresh air
Tickling your neck.
Evil, suffocating monsters coming from every side.
Past bullies destroying your pride.

But what happens if you don't have dreams?
No traumatising past, no delicious ice cream.
You will just be staring into a dark, empty world,
Good thing we don't live in that dream world.

Imani Purnell (12)
ACS International School, Cobham

Imagine If...

Imagine if we were just puppets...
Imagine if we never had a sense of control in life,
Always playing someone else's game,
Not allowed to have a say.
No future ahead of you, no job, no house,
No family because you have no wife.
All you hear from your director's gruff voice is,
"I expect nothing else, just perform your daily play."
You'd get up on stage, all ready and dressed,
While the audience gets seated,
Ready for you to amaze them.
The director pulls out his megaphone
While you wait to be addressed,
The roars and cheers erupt as if you were an expensive gem.
When the show is done and the money pools in,
You stand backstage, sadly watching the crowd leave.
The audience has no idea that you're always so thin,
Because your cruel master
Only lets you feast on something so inedible,
May as well be basket weave.

You spend all your time crying in a corner,
But what if you can change?
Cut the strings that were controlled by that foreigner,
And flee into a world that might be strange.
Find a job that you love,

Buy a house that welcomes you with open arms,
Make some friends so you won't be alone.
Adopt a kid and raise him on a farm.
You give that kid all your love so they would feel at home.
Never bring up that cruel puppeteer, just leave it in the past.
He paid for his sins,
And is now serving time behind bars.
You'd never know how long you'd last,
If you have never been brave enough
To leave and see the stars.

You should never let anyone control you,
Never let anyone hold your strings.
You could spend your time feeling blue,
If you never stood up and spread your wings.

Sanaya Sengupta (13)
ACS International School, Cobham

Imagine If It Was The End Of The World

The end of the world
Imagine, everything was ending
Everything depending
On the smallest of things
Or the biggest, an upper force, pulling on our strings.

All the panic, all the worries
All the manic, crazy flurries
How much would I have to do?
How much to live up to?

There's so much stuff I haven't done
Weighing on my shoulders, more than a ton
I make a list, I check the stopwatch on my wrist
I can taste the tears rolling down my cheek
All the surroundings feel so bleak
Not much time, the big clock chimes
I have to go, I have to do it
I cannot plummet, cannot go into the summits
But I cannot quit, just have to commit.

Live life to the fullest
That's what people tell me
And I wave it away and say
"Don't worry, I have a million days"

But now I look back, it doesn't seem so
It seems that the flow of the days is gone
What I thought was inexorable is now done.

Life is a party
It always comes to a halt, sooner or later
Sometimes a raise of your spirits, sometimes a deflator
I just wish I had listened
My eyes glistened as I thought
Now I have only one day to live life like I should have done
When my life has just begun.

The world is going to end
I have to rush, fit in all the stuff
That I have to do, before the world ends very soon
All the things I've dreamt of doing
All the things I've dreamt of pursuing
Now is the time, the stars bright like the sun
The wind chasing me, now I run
I run to all my dreams
I wish it wasn't what it seems
But the world is ending
The worries extending
The panic ascending
The world is really going to end.

Zahara Nisioti Spyropoulos (12)
ACS International School, Cobham

Imagine If

Imagine if they knew the real you,
The one that powers through,
And thinks you don't have a clue,
But only you know that you do.

Imagine if you make it.
Imagine if you had grit.
Imagine if you were faster than light.
Imagine if you could turn day into night.
Imagine if you were the greatest.
Imagine if you could shoot the ball the straightest.
Imagine if you were a genius.
Imagine if you could fly to Venus.
Imagine if you could swim like a dolphin.
Imagine if you had never fallen.
Imagine if you were the strongest,
With massive muscles all over your body,
With veins bursting out everywhere.
Imagine if you could touch the top of Mount Everest,
Whilst laying on the soft, warm beaches of the Maldives.
Imagine if you could hear the roaring lions in Kenya,
Whilst listening to Santa's reindeer bells on the North Pole.
Imagine if you could see every large and small planet in space.

Imagine if dreams were real,
Little do you know, they are.
You just have to make them a reality.

Oskar Kjellberg (13)
ACS International School, Cobham

My Special Balloon

December 11, 2022,
A balloon that always seemed to remain next to me
Flew away.

I knew the balloon,
Thinly tied to my hand,
Would fly one day,
But I didn't know it would happen
Very soon.

I still remember vividly,
The thinly bound balloon
Escaping from my hand,
Going to the sky.

It was meaningless
To run,
To reach,
To jump.

Tears dripped down
Like rain
Very painfully,
Never stopping.

The balloon gradually got smaller
Like a dot:
Bright,
Enjoying
The sky.

The balloon
Travelled freely
Without pain.

I gently smiled:
The very busy balloon that travelled around the world
Appeared in my dream.

Looking
Healthy,
Lonely.

I wanted to stay
By its side.

I wanted to ask the balloon:
Hello Grandpa, how are you doing?
I know you can't answer my question, but I believe you are doing fine there.
Are you enjoying another new world without any pain? I hope so!
Everyone is missing you a lot.

Can you come to my dream often?

I love you!

Jiwoo Yang (15)
ACS International School, Cobham

Poverty, Everywhere

The homeless and the hungry are found everywhere
There are millions of them out there
The numbers rapidly increasing for every new millionaire
For far too many, life must be unfair
And for others, they can barely make ends meet
It's a struggle all the way
Even so, some are lucky that their bills, they can pay
Some have homes and some have mansions
Which is much more than many can say
The gap between haves and have-nots
Has never been so wide
Their rights and needs have been pushed aside
Not enough to eat, nowhere to sleep, everything is rough
For them, living is tough
150 million in poverty
Tell them how fair life is, and they'll disagree.

Julie Hammer (12)
ACS International School, Cobham

My Flower

A burned flower, gone.
Gone?
One day,
It just came.
Death came.
It looked her in the eye, and dead.
She's dead.

A burned flower, she remains.
She remains with us,
We care.
We love.
We won't forget.
A burned flower, my power, my motivation.

She once was bright and independent.
She stood strong.
With pride.
With passion.

Never will I ever forget her beauty,
Her soul,
Strong.
Strong to the ground,
To the earth,
To her beloved.

I feel it,
Her presence, like how she felt death.
She's here.
Listening,
Looking down from up above.
She sees everything.
Quietly, but she sees.
She knows.
Sometimes she'll hide in the clouds,
But then she'll come back,
She always comes back, like death.
She comes and goes.
Death comes and goes.
One person,
The next.
The next.
It doesn't change.
It won't.
A burned flower, in the sky.
Death, lingering.
Death will come,
And I'll be ready.
Ready to be with my burned flower.

Amalia Poyet (13)
ACS International School, Cobham

Women Are Human

Women. Woe men.
Women are people.
They are human too.
Why do we women feel insignificant then?
Why do we feel like we don't matter?
Is it because we don't?
No!
We are human.
Just like the men,
We have a role and we matter.
When men tell us we look ugly,
To change ourselves,
We listen.
We try to prove,
To prove we are worth them.
But we don't need them to be amazing.
We are letting them own us like a toy.
We aren't toys, are we?
No!
We are human.
So stop letting them,
Letting them control you.
You are better than that.
You deserve so much better than them.
You deserve to be known as an equal.

Yes.
You deserve,
You deserve to be queen.
You shouldn't have to be second,
Like a lower class of human.
You are better.

Mia Blabolil (13)
ACS International School, Cobham

A Voice That Needs To Be Heard

What have the animals done to you?
They have done nothing wrong
But they have remained there,
Suffering from your damage.

Doing
Nothing
Wrong.

Why kill them?
They did not kill you,
They don't deserve it.
So why do you slaughter them?

Your corruption,
Your destruction,
Your devastation
Only hurts them more.
But they do not rebel
Or fight back.
They can't protect themselves from you,
From us.

Why do we attack the defenceless?
They can't cry for help.
Thanks to us, they have no refuge,
No haven,
No home.

What are you doing to save them?
To stop their torture?
To set them free?
Why aren't you helping them?

What have they done to you?

Caitlin Phillips (13)
ACS International School, Cobham

Imagine If

Imagine if you could change an event in history.

Would you stop the world wars,
And the horrible smell of gas outdoors?
Would you stop the Industrial Revolution,
And the sight of all this pollution?
Would you save a dinosaur,
And hear it roar?
Would you change a show,
To soften a blow?

Or would you stop the moon landing,
And all this demanding?
Would you stop global warming,
And all of its storming?
Would you save the oceans,
And all their emotions?
Would you save the world,
If it thirled?

Imagine if you could change an event in history,
Would you do it?

Cooper Bourgeois (12)
ACS International School, Cobham

The Centre Of Attention

Flash, flash, flash!
Over here for one minute, please!
Everyone is following me
Everyone is trying to talk to me
Everyone is trying to look at me
Their stares weigh a thousand tons
And are crushing me like a hydraulic press.

I just wish I wasn't famous like before
Everything has just been so gore
I just want to escape and lay in a meadow by myself
Instead of having wealth.

The cameras are cornering me
The cameras are chasing me
The cameras are controlling me
The cameras have faces
And they have mine.

Ricardo Martinez (12)
ACS International School, Cobham

The Pill

Imagine if contraceptives did not exist,
And all the opportunities women would have missed.
Women can have careers,
And live without fear.

They can also choose not to procreate,
And save up for an estate.
Independence is great,
And what's better is a free state.
The bitter taste of the pill,
Does not fulfil.

Now with this medication,
Women can finish their education.
These tiny white pills,
Give the patriarchy chills.

It's amazing to have choice,
And a voice.
Women can do whatever,
And choose any endeavour.

Renee-Eleanore Schoors (12)
ACS International School, Cobham

Imagine Tottenham Won

Imagine Tottenham won the Premier League
Their team holding the trophy
Imagine Tottenham was fatigued.

Imagine Tottenham tapping
Imagine Tottenham rapping
Imagine Tottenham fans were yapping
Creating a racket in the stadium
Screaming and cheering all night long.

I would not stand
I would not be a fan
I would not like a can
What if that was true?
I would not be a fool
I would not be cruel
And I would keep my cool
Because I know it will never come true.

Matteo Emenalo (13)
ACS International School, Cobham

Life Without Us

Imagine life without humans,
It would be in ruins,
There would be no booms,
There would be no shops,
There would be no drops,
There would be no friends,
There would be no cleanliness.

What would the world be?
How would animals feel?
If there was nothing to help them heal,
Would my clothes be sad,
With no one able to wear them?
And all the gems,
Would be so lonely with nothing to do,
Nowhere to go,
And no place to call home.

Mia Crowther (13)
ACS International School, Cobham

Music

Music is a chance for your soul to be free,
There is no right or wrong,
I can find my soul in a song.
To me, music just flows like a cool summer breeze,
Music is for everyone, it comes with ease.
Music feeds your soul, music puts you at peace.
You should do what frees you,
I say, just do the things you love.
For me, that's music.
Music is what frees me.

Jessica-Heather McDonald
ACS International School, Cobham

The Porcelain Girl

She is their porcelain girl, prisoner to a box of glass.
She sings of power.
They sway to her melody,
Discarding the lyrics, waiting for the chorus,
Nothing to take home and remember.
"Let the foolish dream!" they say. "Let them hope."
How good of them to entertain her fantasy.

She sees the world through their glass,
She can only watch it pass.
Hands too delicate to change anything.
Blood too thin to understand.
She can have her wish on a dandelion,
They have her history written.

But the so-called Fates misjudge her,
Too distracted to notice
How antiquated porcelain figures have become.
They miss the paint flake from their paragon of beauty,
Too pleased by the illusion of falling snow.
They miss the flame of ambition in her eyes,
Starving for success,
Mistaken for an alluring glimmer.
They miss her soul seep out the glass cage,
Leaving a hollow porcelain shell

She covers every wall with her voice,
More firm than melodic.
Her hands mould and shape her future,
One she wants fiercely,
Not wishes for wistfully.
She watches as they dismiss The Porcelain Girl,
Knowing
If they looked past the skin they created for her,
Listened to her words,
Rather than hearing a song,
The potential beating in her body would seem obvious.
They would realise, she is not porcelain at all.

She smiles,
For she clutches the pen.

Emilia Beacham (16)
Bourne Grammar School, Bourne

A Poisonous Delight

A snake upon a tree offers a poisonous delight
Knowing the danger, I still take a bite
And despite the poison slowly spreading
I enjoy the taste of bittersweet blending.

The feeling, the experience of such an angelic demon
That dances with me until the high is gone
That comes again each time I take another bite
And despite his evil, I wish not to fight.

This devil and I both agree
Each time we meet and the poison fills me
Each dance and each deadly kiss
That each time I'm away I dearly miss.

I don't care for the effects of my poisonous treat
As I stand around for us to meet
And each time we do, I lose myself
But I gain some sorrow on my shelf.

The devil and I are like Romeo and Juliet
Till death do us part and we pay our debt
And despite every warning sign
As the poison takes hold, all is fine.

Amy Gardner (15)
Bramhall High School, Bramhall

I Love You

Blood, leaking, pouring, dripping,
Tears running fast down my face.
He held my hands, still leaking his dark, red blood,
The face who once saw and held me,
I know now he shall be forever long gone,
Although he may be gone from the mortal world,
I shall see him again when my death day comes.

Blood, blood, blood,
Nightmares come and go.
In my brain is fear,
I feel like death will never overcome me.
I hope on the day we meet again, I'll be old.
In his heart I know he loves me,
In life or death.
His final words, his last breath,
They didn't have to be about me,
But they were,
"I love you."

Abbie Williams (13)
Bramhall High School, Bramhall

Three

One likes Two
But Two likes Three
Who is Three?

Four likes Five
Or so they say
I think it's just a rumour.

Six is dating Seven
Wait!
Not anymore
On and off all the time
I feel like I need to know more.

Eight cheats on Nine with Ten
But another chance they get
Eleven tells the teachers all the drama
They know even more than me.

But wait!
Exes sit together
I still want to know, who is Three?

We're not even teens.

Twelve is definitely a chav
So is Thirteen
It's all too much.

So many people have had their first kiss
So many on boyfriend three
But who in the world is Three?
Who in the world could it be?

We need to slow down
We need to think
We know the songs
We know all the celebs
There's nothing to hide with the internet now
So who is the mysterious Three?

Olivia Cowan (12)
Bramhall High School, Bramhall

Hopeless

Hopeless, that's how people see the world
A plane of dismay
Hurt and suffering
A delusion of joy, plastered over the cracks.

The fire
That creeps and crawls through the crust
Into the world above
Taking us by full force
Pulling us down
As a fire twists, turns and rolls around
Clawing through the cracks.

The cracks, that just get
Wider
Bigger
Greater
To make more room to claw us in.

Lumps of hatred
Its ash clogging our throat
Till we finally fuel the fire that's clawed us in.

Beady eyes staring at you
The fire swallows you whole.

But people made a hole
They made the dent
They made the crack
That now grows and grows
Swallowing the hope whole.

Elsie Gallo
Bramhall High School, Bramhall

The Power Of Music

Inspired by Jane Austin, 'Without music, life would be a blank to me'.

They laugh,
They stare confused
As to why it can bring euphoria to me.

Yet, his sound is as sweet as honey,
His touch is a flower's petal,
His creativity is a Picasso painting,
His ten soldiers are as powerful as Apollo.

He provided the distraction,
The entertainment at soirees.
He was praised, adored, admired.
He sat and played for hours,
Melancholy melodies between eighty-eight keys.

When I turned double digits
I started, I learned, I fell in love.
It led me to an escape
To a new universe,
An undiscovered part of me now existed.

The vivid memory of hearing, of feeling
Nocturne No. 2 in E-Flat Major
For the very first time.
I drowned in the sound
That filled my broken bones.

My lungs could breathe,
My feet could fly.

It gives my psyche a space,
It gives my soul a voice,
It gives my spirit joy.
I had found my passion,
A masked and lost part of me;
Music.
It provides me with a reason to keep going.

As I dived more and more,
I discovered new jewels,
Like a pirate finding buried treasure.
From Miller to Sinatra to Mercury to the 'Piano Man'.
Their sounds are as sweet as honey,
Their visions are Picasso paintings,
Their passions heard all around the world,
Their talent sold and multiplied.

When one is at a loss for words, the music begins
And takes over.

Grace Gunn (17)
Cokethorpe School, Witney

The Child

The Child lies
Floating.
It lies in space
Weeping.
Its parents have abandoned it
Floating.
Left it
To die.

The Child lies
Floating.
It lies in space
Thinking.
About everything that went
Wrong.
When its parents
Turned toxic.

The Child was once
Full of life.
Covered in it.
Alive itself
For millions of years.
Until its parents
Turned toxic.

The Child was once
Full of life.
Covered in it.
Alive itself.
But its parents grew
Greedy,
Violent,
And cold.

The Child understands.
The Child forgives.
The Child forgives
Where no forgiveness is due.
The parents are wrong,
Guilty,
Of neglect,
Of abuse,
Of murder.

The Child lies
Floating.
It lies in space
Weeping.
Its parents have abandoned it.
The Child was once
Home.
Home to trillions
Over

Its single
Lifetime.

The Child was once
Full of life.
Covered in it.
Alive itself
For millions of years.
Its parents have abandoned it
Floating.
Left it.
To die.

Oscar Luckett
Cokethorpe School, Witney

The Meaning Of A Day

Inspired by Nikita Gill

Each new day brings a brand-new start,
"I'll do it tomorrow," I have time,
That project, that book, that new idea,
"Tomorrow," I say, "trust me, it'll be fine."

Days are short, yet everything can wait 'till the next':
Those twenty-four hours aren't enough for what I want to do
And I don't have the time to read or run;
"Tomorrow," I say, "I'm too busy right now, I thought you knew."

I want to go for a trip or dance and sing,
But there are only 1440 minutes left for that,
No way is that enough, let's just watch TV;
"Tomorrow," I say, "there'll be time then for that."

Let's go to the gym and get other things done,
With 86400 seconds I have the time and feel inspired,
"Let's go!" yet I have homework and chores;
"Tomorrow," I say, "I'm just too tired."

Florence Adepoju (17)
Cokethorpe School, Witney

I May As Well Have Been A Cat

I may as well have been a cat.
A fat
snarling
mound
of fur and flesh,
by the way they looked at me.

I yelled a withering command,
but Cerberus,
with a dozen eyes that flashed shards of primordial poison,
with teeth that curved in -
rotted tegha, putrid scimitar -
no longer heeled
or
obeyed.

A pack,
perfectly poised.
The crooks in their necks
like a shooter's
in the hunt.

I saw my gouges,
pieces missing
of my soon-to-be carrion.

I saw my blood like an oil slick,
flint among the fine sands.

I may as well have been a cat,
by the way they looked at me.

Dee Biles (17)
Cokethorpe School, Witney

The Bubble

I feel happy, most days,
But during some, I become unaware.
Of this bubble consuming me, drowning me,
In sorrows.
Why, I do not know,
But I know I must help myself.
Yet I cannot seem to tell others,
In my mind, thinking they will call me different.
So, I look for that person,
That one person,
Who lifts my mood so high I think I may fall without them.
And they are there, in my mind,
But not there for me in life,
Knowing they do not care for me as much as I do them.
If only they saw me the same as I saw them,
This bubble might go away.
Pop maybe,
But shall always haunt me.

Serafina Conlon-Sangster (14)
Cokethorpe School, Witney

Trust

Hours spent and time put in
To build this house we call trust.

Then one
Word
Look
Movement
And it's gone.
It's destroyed.
Nothing but dust.

All that is left are the memories, broken walls and ruins
Heartbreak, pain and regret.
But you're also left with new foundations
The chance to build something new and something hopeful
To grow, repair and love
This time, not just a house
A home.
For yourself.

Jordyn Everett (16)
Cokethorpe School, Witney

My Citadel In The Sky

My citadel in the sky,
Hidden by smog and mist,
Not a single tear drives by,
With every rip and every twist.

My fortress above the land,
Lock and shut your every door,
But with the touch of a broken hand,
I spy you in the light once more.

Come see us shining at the top,
Once the faint fog clears,
Amidst every creak and every pop,
Guard my mind against mortal fears.

Oh - bullied, bruised, battered, brilliant,
Upon the bark on which I laid you,
Oh - broken, bombed, blasted, beautiful,
Upon the stone with which I made you.

Fly, flutter, flap your wings,
I'll banish every croak and cry,
Simply a puppet pulled by strings,
My citadel in the sky.

Anish Srikanth (16)
Heckmondwike Grammar School, Heckmondwike

Innocent But Guilty

The long-dead inside cry
That only one being can hear
Inside them bears the painful wry
That rare people can bear.

The loudest pound sounds in their hearts
When the judge says guilty
Their faces write despair
That no one can repair.

Crying out loud the opposite words of the judge
But why bother to budge
When no one shall believe?
The pain feels like grief.

Planting many seeds
But not one accepts to grow
They even thought of giving bids
Some even thought of using the bow.

Their heart chanting innocent
Just needed one seed
To believe he is not what he is
And try to make the world realise.

While the guilty goes scot free
The innocent gets the scars
While the guilty enjoys in bars
Justice should be served!

Chibueze Richard Ezebor (13)
Hetton Academy, Houghton Le Spring

Refractions Of Regret

I tap, and I press,
Alphabet craters on my screen; but I digress,
"I'm not sure," I say, but they'd beg and they'd be proud.
Who am I if I do not please the crowd?

An encore; like torrents of comets, they plead,
I provide, and let them tie the leash;
A star, they say? Could I truly be worthy of such a spotlight?
I suppose, if I tried.
"What if you just died?"

"You look stunning," to which I swoon,
Exposed, was it too soon?
My second thoughts; replaced by the first's addiction.
I attempt to combat orbit but I am stopped by unjust friction.

Run, I might,
But I stop, in plight,
To give them insight;
Into a new kind of pleasant night.

The girl in the mirror is not so,
But the young boy of insecure past;
The years went by so fast.
Didn't I want them to last?

My missing childhood; stolen by promised good.
Encore! Encore! They cheer,
Returning to the stage in fear,
The usual, "You're stunning, dear."

Reverberates in my ear.

Evan Lidster (16)
Hetton Academy, Houghton Le Spring

My Sweet Hyacinth

My beautiful angel, we play in the fields,
Chestnut curls dance in the breeze,
Your broken skull, still laying unhealed.
Poor fallen flower, laying with the trees.

The west winds of envy,
He watches you wither.
I failed to save you in the excruciating frenzy.
I watch your fragile, mortal life force slither.

Love of my life,
You were taken too soon.
The memory stabs me in the chest, like a knife,
That terrible day in June.

I tried everything to save you,
I will love you always, and for that, I will endeavour.
My sweet Hyacinth, know that it's true,
My memory of you will live forever.

Isabelle Coleman (12)
King Edward VI School, Lichfield

Love For You

You're blinding me with your beauty
And drawing me in with those eyes.
Your voice is calm but your temper is not.
You will soon be mine.
The future that you are holding will change in seconds,
But the future that you want will change in minutes.
No matter what you say, I will always be looking for you.
No matter what you do, I will always love you.
No matter where you end up, I will always be falling for you.
The things you say to me, make me want to go crazy.
The things you give to me, I will always keep.
The secrets you tell me, I will never forget.
Your strength is surprising to see
And your emotions are amazing to see.
No matter if you laugh or cry,
You will never be able to cover
The beauty that shines underneath.
Your voice is soothing and your eyes are like the open sea,
Your touch is soft and gentle, your lips are just amazing.
Amazing things are what you always do
And terrible things are what you never do.
You are not a human, but an angel that stands before me,
An angel that I will always believe in.
The things you say are never lies
But always the truth that hides,

I will believe you even if you are in the wrong.
I am always watching you, always wanting you,
And always needing you.
You will be mine; you don't have a choice.

Samantha Parkin (14)
King Edward VI School, Lichfield

Nico's The GOAT

One, two, three and to the four,
Nico just won, the super Ballon d'Or,
Used to be Messi,
And Ronaldo,
Now we say Nico is,
The GOAT,
Mbappé's gonna cry,
He has no hairline,
Neymar's looking shy,
He's straightening his tie,
Boring,
Nico is scoring,
This is getting boring,
The Ballon d'Or is calling.

One, two, three and to the four,
Nico just won, the super Ballon d'Or,
Messi's very short,
Ronaldo's getting old,
Nico is the GOAT,
He's flexing on his boat.

One, two, three and to the four,
Nico just won, the super Ballon d'Or,
Everyone's looking scared,
They are all getting prepared,

Students do a quiz,
The Ballon d'Or is his.

One, two, three and to the four,
Nico just won, the super Ballon d'Or!

Nico Girzynski (12)
Little Heath School, Tilehurst

Poverty Makes Me Angry!

Those who do not stand strongly with finance,
Seen to be put down for something that's not their fault.
Shop prices are rising, why so much for heating,
Or to keep the TV on.
We're only human,
Yet most of us have to work multiple shifts
Just to get baby food?
Tell me how this is okay, how you can let this slide,
Evicting people, really?
They only missed the due date by a day!
They have children, some young, some old.
School uniform isn't cheap, neither are textbooks.
How do you expect them to learn
When their parents have to prioritise?
A warm home or education?
Food or pens and pencils?
Clean and new clothes or water?
Why make them choose?
This is what poverty does to people
So why is it still an issue?

Daisy Kinton (14)
Little Heath School, Tilehurst

Manipulation

Manipulation, that's a whole other game,
But for starters, it's far from okay,
It angers me knowing people are used
And betrayed for others' personal gain.
We live in a world where people choose to help themselves
And leave others in the dust,
It makes others worry
Who's actually right and who's done wrong.
Trust is gone, bonds are broken,
What victims go through is sometimes unspoken.
We are not your pawns in your bigger game,
And we're not your puppets or marionettes
In your little puppet showcase.
Leave us alone, we're not doing what you want,
This is our stand against your greed and wrongs!

Zimal Mansur
Little Heath School, Tilehurst

AI Fart

AI art, AI art, AI fart
AI art, AI art, AI fart
AI art is rising, while proper art dies
They say it won't be replaced, they all lie
AI art is rising, while proper art dies
They say proper art can survive, they all lie
AI art, AI art, AI fart
AI art, AI art, AI fart
AI art is taking over
Hopes of proper art sink lower
AI art is taking over
The art ship sinks lower
AI art, AI art, AI fart
AI art, AI art, AI fart.

Laszlo Grant-Roberts (18)
Little Heath School, Tilehurst

Pretty

Pretty is the one thing I wish not to be called,
Why should my personality be belittled by the way I look?
I don't care if I look different,
I don't care if you think I'm weird,
How I am on the outside is not me on the inside,
For on the inside, I'm myself,
Which to you may be colourful, loud and obnoxious,
But the one thing I wish not to be is the word 'pretty'.

Lara Hutt
Little Heath School, Tilehurst

Forever As One

Roses are red,
Violets are blue,
Me and you,
Forever as one,
Rewriting the stars,
Besties for life,
And never stopped trying,
From the day we met,
To the day we die.

Roses are red,
Violets are blue,
Me and you,
Today and forever,
As long as I live,
I will never stop loving you.

Evelyn Card
Little Heath School, Tilehurst

The Void

Haiku poetry

Staring at the void
Darkness stretching far away
Endless black downwards

Staring down below
Stars light the depressing void
In an endless sleep.

Albert Maslewski
Little Heath School, Tilehurst

Luna

O France, although you sleep
We call you, we the forbidden!
The shadows have ears,
And the depths have cries.

Bitter, gloriless despotism
Over a discouraged people
Closes a black thick grate
Of error and prejudice.

It locks up the loyal swarm
Of firm thinkers, of heroes,
But the Idea with the flap of a wing
Will part the heavy bars.

And, as in ninety-one,
Will retake sovereign flight,
For breaking apart a cage of bronze
Is easy for a bronze bird.

Darkness covers the world,
But the Idea illuminates and shines;
With its white brightness, it floods
The dark blues of the night.

It is the solitary lantern,
The providential ray;
It is the lamp of the Earth
That cannot help but light the sky.

It calms the suffering soul,
Guides life, puts the dead to rest;
It shows the mean the gulf,
It shows the just the way.

In seeing in the dark mist
The Idea, love of sad eyes,
Rise calm, serene and pure,
On the mysterious horizon.

Fanaticism and hatred
Roar before each threshold,
As obscene hounds howl
When appears the moon in mourning.

Oh! Think of the mighty Idea,
Nations! Its superhuman brow
Has upon it, from now on, the light
That will show the way to tomorrow!

Madison Smith (12)
Merchants' Academy, Bristol

Listen

Humanity begs and grovels at your feet,
Yet you still ignore their cries of woe.
You thrive off of false democracy.
Shall they have the comfort of warmth
Or dine on the finest of gruel?
Here I write with hands of frostbite.

Listen.

We live in freedom forged in chains,
You speak words forged in lies.
You hear no evil, see no evil -
But you speak nothing but evil,
Like the snake that whispers temptations in thine ears,
Your mouths are stained
With the empty promises you fail to illustrate.

Listen.

As the world - our utopia - crumbles at our very feet,
You are more concerned
With whether you will get this month's taxes.
Calloused hands reach, desperate, for the cloth of rebellion.
Heed the warning of those before you.
"Fill me from the crown to the toe top-full
Of direst cruelty!" you cry.
"Pall thee in the dunnest of smoke of hell!" you exclaim.

Heed me! Heed us!
You squeezing, wrenching, grasping,
Scraping, clutching, covetous old sinners.
History will always repeat itself.

Klaus Isom (15)
Merchants' Academy, Bristol

Bullying

One day,
There was a little girl,
Her name was Kay.
And the little girl didn't want to go to school,
Do you want to know why?
Maybe because she was
Getting called names.
Maybe because she
Got called ugly because
Of her friends.
Maybe it made her feel
Like she should die.
But she couldn't
Because she had family to
Take care of, but
One day her house
Was silent and her mum
Walked in.
You would never guess
What she saw:
Blood dripping from the roof, her daughter
Did something
She never thought she would do.

Faith Smith Chivers (12)
Merchants' Academy, Bristol

Valentine

V iolent love, just for me
A nd your face is all I see
L ove me please, if you dare
E xcited I am as people will stare
N obody now can stop my eyes
T onight we will rise
I n this moonlit sky
N othing is worth the view
E xcept you
S miling through the night

D are you might
A sk me now
Y ou are the one I love somehow

Will you be my valentine?
For we can align
These broken pieces
Of our hearts.

Faith Pearce (13)
Merchants' Academy, Bristol

The Better Future

People say, "What do you want to be?"
I reply, "Nothing yet but you will see."
It's okay not to know,
And it's okay to make mistakes.
You can have a vision or future,
Or maybe not,
But if it makes you happy,
Go and do it.
Make your choice.
Be proud of it.
Don't listen to people who don't accept,
Have confidence in what you do,
And have friends who support you.

Jagoda Jastrzebska (13)
Merchants' Academy, Bristol

I'm Tired

Words after words
Kicks, punches, and pain.
Every day is old
Not as new as we are told.
New day, new me
There is no such thing.
My head pounding every morning.
Body aching
Eyes twitching
My brain losing control.
I want to stop pretending
The mask is breaking
And it's tiring.

Jannat Khurram (17)
Merchants' Academy, Bristol

This Is You!

You're not how much you weigh
Or what you choose to wear
You're not your inner thigh gap
Or the way you do your hair
You're not your flabby tummy
Or the bags under your eyes
Your eyebrows are just perfect
And your body size is the right size
You're not your disability
Or fragile mental state
You don't choose to have an illness
And it's not up for debate
You're not your sexuality
Your gender or your race
Your worth has no relation
To who you fall for, or your face
You're all the little pieces
Of the things you see and do
What you learn from what you suffer
Is how you become you
Place weight onto your kindness
Choose love and loyalty
See your realness in the mirror
This is you!

Vendija Graudina (13)
Northampton Academy, Northampton

Climate Change

Leading the fight against climate change,
Lots of obstacles that we will face.
Global warming is coming soon,
But we'll still see the sun and moon.
What about our plants and trees?
Intense droughts, severe fires,
Rising sea levels, melting polar ice,
Declining biodiversity.
Stop global warming!
Climate change won't just impact forests,
Or coral reefs, or even people in far-off
Countries - it will affect all of us.
From more extreme weather to increasing food prices
And gas prices to recreation and decreased
Opportunities to appreciate the natural world,
People everywhere will feel its effects.

Adam Sobocinski (12)
Northampton Academy, Northampton

Kindness

Kindness will never cost you anything,
It will just open up your heart.
Kindness will always stay with you,
So that you will have a perfect start,
Kindness is just a simple act,
You don't need to pay,
So just smiling at someone could really
Make their day,
My parents always taught me to be kind to others,
So that other people would pass it on to others,
You see, this is how kindness is spread,
Like Princess Diana once said,
"Carry out a random act of kindness,
With no expectation of a reward,
Safe in the knowledge that one day,
Someone might do the same for you."

Natalia Stanciulescu (11)
Northampton Academy, Northampton

If My Pup Could Prattle

If my pup could prattle, I think he
Would have a lot to say,
He would probably say to my mum,
"Don't go out, please stay."
He would definitely say to my dad,
"When are you buying more food?"
And he would say to my brother,
"Leave me alone, I'm not in the mood."
He would say to my grandma,
"If I give you my paw."
And a lick for Grandad and ask,
"Will you spoil me even more?"
And finally, he would say to me,
"I love you the most in our family."
And I would reply,
"Same here, you're my best buddy."

Riyan Unadkat (12)
Northampton Academy, Northampton

Lighthouse

Dark and alone in a bleak abyss is where I stood,
My rusty, rotten exterior made of wood,
I was abandoned by a dear old friend,
Now I fear it may be my end,
Surrounded by the aggressive crashing of my enemy below,
The fierce attack of a fatal blow,
I hope that someday my kind will thrive,
But this time I believe I should take a dive,
Down a tunnel, so my relatives can survive,
My story might have taken a traumatic turn,
"Why?" you ask,
This is a story to promote the future,
Soon, in the new world, I will reappear,
When the time is right.

Tamara Floszmann (13)
Northampton Academy, Northampton

Grow

The day I could no longer walk with ease,
Without more disease,
It became clear to me that I was growing,
I could see above the window, far out,
Into a world of doubt,
Where children yearned to grow and be about.

When I achieved tall stature I would know,
Those peaks of knowledge held below,
All that reminded me to do was grow,
Yet wisdom gained shows ahead,
Grown up, I find I'm growing down instead.

Millie Laugharne (12)
Northampton Academy, Northampton

You're One In A Million

You're one in a million, my most special one
Your amazing smile as bright as the sun
You're smart and caring and have many
great charms
I'm only happy and fine when I'm in your arms
I'm happy you've chosen me from all the rest
Now I'm proud 'cause I know I've got the best
You are so cute and sweet, and you are my world
I love you so much, my most beautiful girl!

Sophie Clarke (11)
Northampton Academy, Northampton

Winter Miracle

Bright lights shine in the night,
What a beautiful sight!
Christmas decorations on the doors.
Father Christmas flying high,
Delivering presents all night,
Bringing happiness all night round.
Outside, children playing in the snow,
Building snowmen using carrots for the nose,
Pebbles and rocks for the eyes and mouth.

Nikola Izosina (11)
Northampton Academy, Northampton

Stand Up For Ukraine

Whilst we are all safe at night, snuggled up in our beds,
In Ukraine, there is a war going ahead,
With bombs going off, left, right and centre,
Ukraine stands together to fight and not surrender.

What is the point of war anyway?
To make people scared and leave them in pain?
We should all be equal and work out things together,
Without all the suffering that goes on forever.

What can they do but hope and pray all day?
Whilst they sit on a cramped plane going far, far away,
It is awful for them, and they had no clue,
Until they heard the loud noises that grew and grew.

Imagine packing a bag and being told you need to flurry,
Out of your hometown and to do it in a hurry,
Leaving behind everything you've ever known,
Wondering if you'll ever go back to the place you call home.

So, when you are annoyed or don't get your own way,
Stop for a second, do what I do and say,
I have an incredible life, really, I do,
As there are people in Ukraine who would kill to be you.

Eleanor Garlick (13)
Ormiston Rivers Academy, Burnham-On-Crouch

I Am Your Home

I am your home,
But you destroy,
My skin and bone,
But I forgive,
And I forget,
And let you live,
But I regret.

Do you realise,
I am your only hope,
So don't stand around and mope,
I need saving,
It's up to you,
This is what I need you to do.

No more plastic,
And no more waste,
Because I am fading at a fast pace,
I need love,
I need care,
Because you are polluting my air...

Thomas Yates (13)
Ormiston Rivers Academy, Burnham-On-Crouch

Insolence And Ignorance

Silenced evermore
But quiet no longer
Ignored where love may not be found
And in themselves
All hope lies buried
Where wasteful war
Shall allies overturn
Live like this
And prosper in the devil's eyes
The spirit of ignorance
With a perpetual dullness
But dismantled mortality o'ersways
With power
A never-ending death
A life I did not choose
But my mortality deserved
So I no longer mourn my freedom.

Georgie Cordell (12)
Pipers Corner School, Great Kingshill

Stick War: Legacy

"**S** ummon the Elite," the wise old man said,
 T urned out to be the wise Magikill of the head,
 I namorta stood, as the Magikill approached,
 C rowded King Atreyos, asking tactics, he broached,
"**K** ing Atreyos, your task is to vow, not to be a cockroach."

W ar had struck, his Speartons and Archidons,
A ll at once, his men had gone,
R ivalry against the boss, him and giants.

L eg was where his wound leant,
E verywhere sprawled, his men who'd been hunted,
G ave up but the wise Magikill spawned in his last breath.
A t last, big fleets of Swordwrath arrived but came upon his death,
C rowded the battlefield, surrounding the enemy,
Y ield, they had done, then there was peace.

Dylan Marcelo (11)
Priory Academy, Dunstable

My Nana

The day you left me is the day I will never forget.
November the 1st 2019.
The memories will never be forgotten.
The way your smile widened when we saw you.
The way you made Pops laugh.
The way you were always bossy.
The way you told Dad off when he was doing something he shouldn't.
You ate Polos like they were the love of your life.
You cooked like a professional chef.
We always called the sausages Nana's special sausages.
But now we can't call them that anymore.
Your chair is now taken by my brother.
He always says, "Can I sit in Nana's chair?"
It's always a yes.
Whenever I come to your grave it hurts, it really does.
I never thought I would lose you.
Nobody thought that we would lose you.
Your laugh lit up the whole world.
Your happiness filled the room with joy.
Your advice will never be forgotten.
The way you would let me light the candles when it was the Jewish Passover.
The way you made your sweet bread.
Now I try to remake your honey cake to carry the tradition on.

I carry you in my heart every day.
Rest in peace Nana.

Alice Bijum (14)
Priory Academy, Dunstable

Running For Fun?

This is my poem of fun
Air pushing me back
But I like to run
So I sweat short breaths
Quickly pushing me far
Legs in the air
It ain't getting me there.

Because underneath all of this
There is a random raw heart
Beating and breathing
It needs some love.

Am I running for something
Or running from something?
Perhaps I'm running for fun
Or running for nothing.

Hair pulled back in a little tight bun
Pressure's applied
But I'm feeling light
'Cause the fear is greater
But I'm running faster.

From the Earth
Which is giving birth to Mother Nature
But the rapture
It's coming soon
Signs of the world's destruction
Global warming
Sadly swarming.

But it's whatever
'Cause as long as I'm alive
Then I'll really rely
On the government, right?

'Cause I'm not living in the remains of the world
I'll leave that here for my latter little pearls.

Armani Musamadya (13)
Priory Academy, Dunstable

Our World

Our world is stunning,
Our world is upbeat,
But most importantly it is our home,
To fight for as long as we are alive,
This is a world that is worth fighting for.

This world has brought pleasure to every being living on this world,
However, our world is soon to stop producing its natural flame,
Because of us!
Pollution, deforestation, greenhouse gases, droughts, global warming,
To name a few.

This was all done by us and now we have to fix it until it is too late,
This world has so much to offer us in the future and we are leaving it,
To be cleaned up by our future generations, it is our time to clean up our predicament,
This world gave us a gift a home, now we have to give it our gift,
Sustainability.

Ryan Brimmell (13)
Priory Academy, Dunstable

Brother And Sister

Bro and sis, we always had fun
And in the middle of the night
You would sneak around and give me a fright
And there were times when I would hide
And you would look for me high and wide.

But then the time struck
My brother's back hurt so much he couldn't go up the stairs
We went to the hospital and found out he had a tumour
I was frightened and sad as
We had some of the best times when he came into my room
For no reason and dragged me out
So we could play Spider-Man on his PlayStation.

He chose to go through surgery
And this could cause him to die
But he survived
And that was the time my elder brother nearly died.

Meghan Morris (11)
Priory Academy, Dunstable

EB Lions AFC

Saturday league football is the GOAT
I always have to wear my coat
Aidan's grandad owns a boat
Aidan Kenna is the GOAT
I ate a pork pie
That is no lie
We got super Dan
Hits me on the head with a pan.

Lucas Bidaudville-Begley (12)
Priory Academy, Dunstable

Our Planet

Going outside for fresh air can be a deadly breeze,
Whilst you're reading this an animal's home is being seized,
The sea levels are rising but no one really cares,
Just because you can't see it doesn't mean it's not there,
Climate change is hurting others behind all the screens,
We need to recycle but ignorant people refuse,
You see it all on telly and call it 'fake news',
Little do you know you're the one who is causing the murderous plumes.

The time is ticking very fast,
We need to save our planet before none of us last,
They've left it to our generation to clean up their mistakes,
But they need to help us with all the troubles that await,
Thick clouds of smoke billow into the sky,
All the animals are being tortured while the government lie,
They tell us that they'll fix it and everything will be okay,
But on our floor is where all the litter lays.

Pollution surrounds our planet every day,
How did we let it get this way?
Think about all the rubbish you abuse,
And how you could reduce, recycle and reuse,
We swim in dirty water when we could be relaxing in a crystalline sea,
If we all acted now, came together and agreed,
We could live in a happy and healthy world, indeed.

Kiara
Ridgeway Academy, Welwyn Garden City

The World

The world.
The world is so powerful, so masterful, so delightful,
The people that live in the world are hopeful,
It's like one big ball,
That isn't referred to as small,
The world may seem nice but isn't what it may seem,
The seas are not clean,
The land is not clean,
The *world* is not clean.

Pollution.
Pollution is one key thing,
Litter,
Litter, everywhere,
It just seems like no one cares,
We need to be mindful, thoughtful, careful,
We only have one world,
We need to protect it.

Power.
Power is strong,
But can sometimes be wrong,
It is controlling, mindblowing,
It can take control and put you in a negative role,
Power is needed to rule and keep charge,
People who are large and small like to protest and barge.

The future.
In the future there will be lots of happiness,
Happiness is all around us,
There will be no badness,
The future may behold something that is unexpected,
But sometimes can be detected,
Our world today may seem dull,
But, in the future, I see green,
It will be filled with green and won't be mean,
In my mind, there won't be any litter,
Or people that are bitter,
Our world will be perfect,
It will be just like a candy bowl filled with sherbet.

Change.
What would I change?
I would change homelessness,
So that people have a place to stay without having to pay,
It is unfair that people have to stay cold,
But other people go into their homes and stay, behold.

Our world is lovely after all,
It is our home,
One big ball.

Kaysie Davies (12)
Ridgeway Academy, Welwyn Garden City

Growing Older

When we are all young most of us wish to grow older quickly.
To have responsibilities, jobs and most importantly to be listened to and heard.
Yet in reality, it's scary growing up.
You have expectations and beauty standards.
It's not all bad though.
You don't get treated like a baby anymore and you get a say in different things, but there is something about growing up that is frightening or almost intimidating.
As teenagers or adults, we find growing up isn't always magical as we imagined.
It is fraught with the disappointments and challenges that are a necessity to becoming a mature person.

Growing up can be described as a roller coaster, many ups and downs, twists and turns, but everything will be okay in the end.
It can bring many anxieties yet it can be some of the best times in your life.
As a teenager, you're almost free in a way.
You get to go out with your friends at the weekend and you can enjoy your hobbies.
But growing up isn't just about growing taller or not being able to run as fast as you could when you were younger, it's about growing stronger.
Learning to not beg for what you want but instead to get what you need.

Growing up can also be a time of discovery, wonder and freedom, so don't wish your life away.
Relax and enjoy it for you will almost blink and it will be over and you won't regret being bubbly and joyful in your teenage years.

Elizabeth Dawson (11)
Ridgeway Academy, Welwyn Garden City

Good Mood Food

It was a cold day
In the middle of May
The clouds were moving fast in the sky
And there was one fly
The fly buzzed around looking for food
Food to fix his bad mood
But the shop doors were closed
So, he flew further down the road
Where the market stalls were also closed
He flew further along the road
Where he saw a man eating a sandwich
He buzzed around the sandwich and looked at it with glee
The fly thought to himself *this sandwich is for me*
So, he thought of a plan
To trick the man and get his delicious food
The food that he needed to fix his bad mood
So, he thought and thought for a long while
But that while was too long
And the man's sandwich was gone
"Oh no, where did the sandwich go?"
The hungry fly looked around for the delicious sandwich
But it was nowhere to be seen
There were lots of rumbles coming from the fly's stomach
And he looked around for food
He searched and searched through the town

And he was shivering and hungry
Much more than before
He turned around and saw a sandwich shop
So, he flew in through the window
And saw delicious sandwiches everywhere
He licked his lips and found one to eat
So, he ate and ate and his bad mood finally was gone.

Bella Flaherty (12)
Ridgeway Academy, Welwyn Garden City

Music

Music, the key to everyone's heart
The sound that brings us all together
It's the one friend that will never depart
The potion to feeling as light as a feather.

From going on a jog
To climbing to the top
It makes you restart until you drop
Feeling as tired as a flip-flop.

Music, the key to everyone's heart
The story that will never end
It's the one friend that will never depart
Indeed, it will make you feel on trend!

Like wearing Adidas or Nike
On a long family hike
Or cooling down on a warm summer day
Indeed, you'll need a speaker to hear it that way.

Music, the key to everyone's heart
Something to be easily declared
It's the one friend that will never depart
And this is something that should always be shared!

Jonnell Mbangu
Ridgeway Academy, Welwyn Garden City

Save The Sea Creatures

Watching the smoke stacks choke the sky,
Always made me want to cry,
I just can't help but wonder why,
The factories won't even try,
To find a safer, better way,
To put their poisonous waste away.

The coral reefs are dead or dying,
If fish could cry they would be crying,
The pollution we caused has taken a toll,
But yet we sit around and have a nice stroll.

The plastic, oils and more,
How could the planet expect what we had in store?
Humans think that they are so genius,
But all of our inventions are for our own convenience.

The turtle population went down,
Because humans leave their rubbish all over town,
Now all you need to do is recycle,
Then you will have a nice view when riding your bicycle.

Harriet Jones (11)
Ridgeway Academy, Welwyn Garden City

My Climate Change Poem!

The rainforests are getting destroyed
The animals are losing their homes
Our futures are disappearing
And it's time to take action
The planet is dying
It makes me feel like crying.

The rhinos are losing their horns
They're stealing the elephants' tusks
Murdering innocent animals
And it's got to stop
The animals are dying
It makes me feel like crying.

The seas are becoming a dumping ground
For plastic, rubbish and filth
It's killing coral reefs and sea creatures
We need to protect our world
The oceans are dying
It makes me feel like crying.

The icebergs are melting quickly
And the seas are warming up
Our world is going to flood
And we must act now to save us all

Our home is dying
It makes me feel like crying.

George Rhodes
Ridgeway Academy, Welwyn Garden City

January's Ice

Today the ice bit me,
It hurt, so I said,
"Please go away,
I hate the slippiness,
And you're to blame,"
But the ice just bit me,
Faster and harder,
Swirling around,
And out from the icy breeze,
A deep voice croaked,
"January may be cold,
Icy and misty,
You may be scarred by it,
Feel hard from it,
And feel discarded by it,
But without January,
Who will start off the year with a bang?
But without January,
Who will start a new beginning?
But without January,
As your adversary,
Who will look forward to summer?"
So, you may be scarred by it,
Feel hard from it,
And feel discarded by it,

But there is always hope,
That summer will come soon.

Chloe Thompson (12)
Ridgeway Academy, Welwyn Garden City

The Zoo

Today we went to the zoo
The sky was a bright shade of blue
When we first entered
I stopped and presented
A wonderful, magical zoo.

In this sensational zoo
There were monkeys that looked just like you!
We stopped and we listened
As the otter pools glistened
To the sound of this magical zoo.

In this astonishing zoo
An elephant looks at you
He leans out his trunk
But it's filled up with gunk
This strange but tremendous zoo.

We were near the end of the zoo
The sky was no longer blue
We should come again
With our other friend, Len
To this outstanding, crazy, big zoo.

Eva Harrison (11)
Ridgeway Academy, Welwyn Garden City

What Am I?

I am comfortable and enticing,
I wonder where my unconsciousness will take me,
I hear creaks and squeaks,
I see a fortress of dreams,
I am comfortable and enticing.

I feel halcyon,
I touch a plush menagerie,
I worry about time,
I cry out,
I want this forever,
I am comfortable and enticing.

I need this to function,
I need this to stay healthy,
I need this for my well-being,
I need this to perform,
I need to do this for one-third of my day,
What am I?

Answer: My bed.

Finn Stratton
Ridgeway Academy, Welwyn Garden City

Emotions

I promise you he notices
He notices that you go out of your way and do little things for him
He picks up on the little ways you try and improve his day
Or how when he talks you always have a big smile on your face and a glimmer in your eye
He notices that you laugh extra hard when it's him who makes the bad jokes
He isn't oblivious to your feelings for him
But the problem is he just doesn't want it to be you
He pursues the girl that does not have the same emotions as you.

Jojo Laci (15)
Ridgeway Academy, Welwyn Garden City

Cost Of Living Crisis

Prices go up
Meaning an empty plate and cup
Families can't afford to eat
Even the cheapest cut of meat.

There is help which is a never-ending task
But families are often too afraid to ask
Food banks and charities are always there
Providing food, drink and welfare.

Spread the word about help, it's not too hard to find
Let's all come together to support all mankind
Lend a helping hand when you can
It's kind and you'll be their greatest fan.

Lois Grostrate (11)
Ridgeway Academy, Welwyn Garden City

Musical Harmony

Without music in my life where would I be?
It brings out so many emotions in me.
It can make you feel happy or make you feel sad
It can tell stories of good and stories of bad.
It can evoke memories from the past
And bring them to the present to make them last.
It can remind us to smile, cry, move and be free
And it helps to bring out the best in me.
Without music my mind would be hectic
I feel blessed that I'm musically eclectic.

Dylan Bragg (12)
Ridgeway Academy, Welwyn Garden City

The World

Look at our world today,
We see beauty and life,
But it wasn't always like this.

Roses were red,
Violets were blue,
People used to say God made us beautiful,
What happened to you?

There was violence,
There were arguments,
And punches and crunches,
And not a lot of glue.

Now we are civil,
In a civilisation we share and care for,
Love and do dares for.

Amie Davies (12)
Ridgeway Academy, Welwyn Garden City

War

Desolate land, no soldiers left
Bloodstained bodies in uniforms
Loyal to their country to serve and protect
Many lost their lives fighting for freedom
They mourn as they remember the ones they have lost
Cold, bitter memories of war remain
Lifeless bodies are scattered amidst the poppy yards
Cruel war brings heartache and tears
There, their final breaths were taken
Until their lives were blown away like the petals of a poppy.

Ranulya Kotalawela (12)
Ridgeway Academy, Welwyn Garden City

Hemsby

To the East of England where the sun always shines,
Hemsby is there, never saying goodbye,
Hemsby is a lovely place to be,
And there are loads of fun things to do and see.

All the people are lovely and everyone loves to go to the beach,
And coastal walks are easy to reach,
There are baby seals that are cute and playful,
People should be grateful,
To be in this beautiful place,
Where everyone always has a smile on their face.

Summer St John
Ridgeway Academy, Welwyn Garden City

The Cycle Of The Seasons

As December ends,
And January ascends,
We look towards the year.

The frost's here now,
And the dark nights in tow,
We await for it all to clear.

As the blossom blooms,
And the earthy rain falls
All the new life,
Starts beginning to crawl.

The sun is now shining,
The dark days are done,
Now it is time to go have some fun.

The leaves are all rustling,
Brown, yellow and red,
The dark days are coming all over again.

Cassie Messer
Ridgeway Academy, Welwyn Garden City

Potatoes

Straight from the soil,
Should I boil?
I prefer mashed,
Never hashed,
Cut into chips,
Served with dips,
Or maybe the little discs,
They call crisps,
How about toasted?
Actually, I'd like them roasted,
Jacket potato with beans and cheese,
Or with gravy and peas,
I'd like all of these please,
Sweet potatoes are orange,
New potatoes are white,
In a salad or in an oven,
Potatoes themselves are purely a delight.

Willow Beer (11)
Ridgeway Academy, Welwyn Garden City

Green

Each morning I wake up in the same prison,
And see the sight of the emerald-green walls
That enclose my room from the vast, green wilderness.
Down my sage-green stairs are more enclosed, prison-cell-like rooms,
Each has a different hue of green staining its plaster walls.
Everywhere I go I see the same tranquil colour,
Even the people around me are green with envy.

Jayden Benford (11)
Ridgeway Academy, Welwyn Garden City

Football

Football is a beautiful game.
Football, followed by most.
Football, the atmosphere of the stadium gives you goosebumps.
Football, we play, we watch, we love.
Football, not one by one but team by team.
Football, the clubs, the stadium, the fans all as one.
Football, the skills, the pass, the shot and the *goal!*
Football, we play, we watch, we love.

Rhys Stratton
Ridgeway Academy, Welwyn Garden City

Joule Pool

Joule was brave,
Always going to the high waves.
Her last name was Pool,
And the colour of the water was azul.
She loved seeing the water ripple,
But she always had to pay a few nickels.
People always found her enthusiastic,
But she would always be sarcastic.
Although she hated school,
Her name was Joule Pool.

Rafael Hilario (11)
Ridgeway Academy, Welwyn Garden City

Lazy Daisy

Lazy Daisy
She sleeps for days
And has her ways
I know her well
This girl can't spell
No wonder why she isn't clever
Her brain is the size of a feather
This life is a big lie
Many of her friends said goodbye
I'd like to help her a lot
But she is not hot.

Frank Rozanek (11)
Ridgeway Academy, Welwyn Garden City

The Power Of Poetry

As sweet as a blossom
As smart as a possum
My friend, you are one of a kind
You have a thoughtful mind
Always there for me
An amazing part of society
Our friendship will never end
Even if we turn a bend
A really great friend for me
The best friend a person could be.

Brandon Paterson (12)
Ridgeway Academy, Welwyn Garden City

Art

I love art because it's inside my heart
Experimenting with cool colours to restart
To design things to sparkle and to tell a beautiful story
That makes it look like glory
I like to draw cute animals that look really real.

Isabella Staines (11)
Ridgeway Academy, Welwyn Garden City

Power Of Poetry

F riends forever
R elationships
I ncredible connection
E asy-going
N ever-ending
D ebonair
S uccessful
H elpful
I ncredible
P owerful.

Lexi Gorman
Ridgeway Academy, Welwyn Garden City

Sad Chad

He was always mad,
And people said it was because of his dad,
His name was Chad,
And he was always sad,
He had tears dripping out of his eyes,
Sometimes he was very wise,
He loved his home,
And he collected gnomes,
His name was Sad Chad.

Jayden Clarke
Ridgeway Academy, Welwyn Garden City

Help The Homeless

We need to support the people who are

- **H** elpless
- **O** ut of work
- **M** iserable
- **E** nduring mistreatment
- **L** onely
- **E** xhausted
- **S** tarving
- **S** uffering

In our society.

Cameron Burt (12)
Ridgeway Academy, Welwyn Garden City

Pollution

The world is being destroyed by pollution
It isn't caused by a train station
It comes from factories around the world
Global warming should be heard
This needs to be stopped soon
We need to get the Earth in tune.

Joshua Masson (12)
Ridgeway Academy, Welwyn Garden City

Await

I sat there in the abyss
A cold and dark nothingness
No emotion but fear.

Then there was a light
A light white and bright
Hope.

A garden
A place to breathe
The people I love.

My friends
My family
My home.

Eleanor McDonald (12)
Ridgeway Academy, Welwyn Garden City

Stuck

The cold, rough ocean
The sad, worried sea
The breathless, sharp bag
The bag floating and drifting
The turtle not hungry
The hurt and hungry turtle
The confused creature
Why do people let this happen?

Tom Rhodes
Ridgeway Academy, Welwyn Garden City

The Importance Of Earth
A haiku

Beautiful nature
Makes our world more colourful
Earth is important.

Lois Friend
Ridgeway Academy, Welwyn Garden City

Sunny Eventide

A haiku

Sunny eventide
A fantastic tiger moos
In spite of the king.

Jake Vine (12)
Ridgeway Academy, Welwyn Garden City

Hunger It Was

I sat there in silence
Begging for help
As it had been days
That I had not been myself
Hunger it was.

No food on the table
Just loose change in a cup
Sleepless, cold nights it was
As I see people passing by through the night
Not even looking at the conditions we're in
Me and her, her and me
As we longed for something we never had
Hunger it was.

From place to place we moved
The problems were stacking higher than the food
As we got kicked out
Just another daily move
Hunger it was.

She couldn't take it anymore
Her last few words will be remembered
As she took her last breath
She left this world
Because of hunger it was.

As I sit by myself
It's hard to believe that I didn't succeed
One lost someone
Someone that they loved
Because of hunger it was.

Irum Ara (12)
Saltley School, Birmingham

Inflation

Governments ever so cantankerous
Always making moves so ferocious
Cold and dull evenings
The pain and agony every morning.

I wonder why the world is falling apart
But still, even I am not playing my part
I wish I could do more
But I'm just a child, so to me, it is just a bore.

Inflation is causing even more hunger
Because bills are roaring down like thunder
All of our limbs are getting very **cold**
And yes, I especially wrote that in bold
Just imagine inflation rising like the price of gold.

Inflation really dominates
And now I'm trying to contemplate
What will we do if it gets worse?
Is this world truly cursed?

Ayub Isxaaq
Saltley School, Birmingham

Changes

When life goes well there's that change
First railways and buses, what else will change?
Now NHS and teachers
What else can these strikes feature?

It's all about money this, money that
But what about the things that won't last?
There are too many bills they have to pay
Some people can't stay in their place
It's hard to keep up so
Where can this take us?

From this people come and go
Because of that thing that identifies them
They fight for their future
So they don't have to be worried about their colour.

Samuel Abdin (12)
Saltley School, Birmingham

Miss Jones

Miss Jones, I think you must be told,
For a teacher, you're getting rather old.
Saying nothing against you, of course,
But I simply mustn't reveal my source.

You see, all of the other teachers,
Know you have a hard time with the creatures.
Running around you all long day,
Really just leading each other astray.

Perhaps it's time to take a step back,
Before they simply make you crack.
You've been at this school many winters and summers,
Decades longer than most of the others.

Don't pull that face at me, Miss Jones,
Don't make a fuss, no whines and moans.
I always said I'd let you know,
When it was time for you to go.

I know, I know, you could run a mile,
But you wouldn't necessarily do it with style.
I do think it's time for you to retire,
I think that's what you truly desire.

You were a great maths teacher, it's true,
Teaching Year Ones how to add two and two.
And the older children could calculate,
Exactly how old you were, it's been great.

Your history was up to scratch,
A level of detail that no one could match.
Of course, you were around back then,
Were you eleven - or was it ten?

You've taught many thousands and thousands of pupils,
Most of them without any scruples.
But still, you remained perfectly on the rail,
And only a few ended up in jail.

I know it's hard to say goodbye,
But you really must see why.
I have to say these things to you -
Miss Jones, you're 192!

Emmeline Rhodes (11)
Sarah Bonnell School, Stratford

Climate Change Is No Joke

Our problems all began with the industrial revolution
And its legacy has left us with toxic pollution
Climate change is real and has been declared a code red
If we choose to ignore it, we will all end up dead
Ice caps are melting, I am sure you already know
And soon the polar bears will have nowhere to go
Sea levels are a worry as they continue to rise
Houses and cars swept away before our very eyes
Wildfires are quite common now the air is so dry
Many people lose their homes, and sadly many of them die
Our vast oceans too have become a dumping ground
With oil slicks and plastics, just some of the things found
We burn fossil fuels that release carbon to keep us warm
Now we must find an alternative that won't cause us any harm
Pesticides spread on crops with no thought for the bees
Forests cut down ruthlessly, soon there will be no trees
Action is needed now, you know what's needed to be done
Because when it gets worse, there will be nowhere to run
And those people out there who think it's just a big joke
They won't find it so funny when they're choking on smoke.

Lelas Elwan (12)
Sarah Bonnell School, Stratford

Opening Opportunities

Inspired by Latesha, 'When I feel like no one hears me, I just write!'

- **O** pportunity is like opening a door that will lead you to new, mesmerising adventures
- **P** owerful, these doors can be...
- **P** eople are there to help you in your journey of opportunities
- **O** h, there are millions of doors waiting for you to open them
- **R** eady, you have to be to unlock these doors that are shining like gems
- **T** urn each handle, and as you open them, let them blast you with amazing, excellent chances
- **U** ntie your prediction, let yourself try something new
- **N** othing is there to stop you from having fun
- **I** t is going to help you be excited about new things you have never ever done before
- **T** ime will go by and you will soon want to open more...
- **Y** ou just have to open, open and open for new experiences!

Saba Hoque (12)
Sarah Bonnell School, Stratford

Save The Bees

I fly my little wings,
Hoping to be set free,
Of this monstrosity I face every spring,
Deforestation, uprooting plants and a massacre of my fellow bees.

I fly with hope,
Although it is already lost,
My little heart just trying to cope,
Suffering, I have learnt, is now part of life.

Day by day,
I flutter so gently,
From the nefarious today,
As I tolerate in vain.

Work drenches me with misery,
I scavenge further nowadays than I have ever before,
This is all human trickery,
I have been deceived as my queen bee is a hostage.

However, there is a silver lining,
A green meadow of blooming flowers and flourishing flora,
It reaches out to me, shining,
My dreams come true, I see it, I dream it, I feel it,
But where can I find it?

Achievement, ambition, aspiration I see it,
All I have to do is get a leader to achieve it,
There are you humans, I believe you can do this,
We bees will help you if you come and give us a hand through it.

Save the bees.

Angela Tang (12)
Sarah Bonnell School, Stratford

One Broken Planet, One Brighter Future

Cigarettes puff smoke into the infected air
The addictive fumes wafting away freely
A body of plastic slowly sprawls through the city
Obliviously suffocating the sea.

Forty-two million trees are ruthlessly chopped off daily
1.3 million gallons of thick oil are poured into the solemn sea each year
100,000 marine animals die tangled up in our plastic yearly
I wonder who is to blame here?

Our Earth is perishing, day by day
Quaking in endless pain
Exploding in unfathomable agony
Shivering with unsettling fear.

So I believe
I dare to dream
That one day
One day
We humans will step up and make things right
We will get our act together to make a change
We will all believe in ourselves
We can do this!
We can save our Earth

All we need to do is trust each other
Work hard as a team
And indeed,
After the whole world's love and effort
My beautiful Earth will finally be free
Free.

Subaha Saif (13)
Sarah Bonnell School, Stratford

Awareness For Change

What enrages you so much that makes you feel like you have to do something about it?
Climate change.
Global warming.

Things that should already be dealt with.
Why are we the cause of climate change?
Isn't that quite strange?

That we don't do our part of the job?
Who will look after the planet if we don't?
Don't think the planet will manage everything itself because it certainly won't.

We are like a disease, aren't we?
Can't you see?
There is no cure!

There will never be a cure until we do something!
You know, we will be affected by global warming just as much as the Earth is.
The Earth will not stay green and blue forever in this state.

As trees slowly die, so will we.
We can not hide from climate change
We can not run from climate change.

We need to mend the Earth's heart!
We need to do something.
Before it's too late...

Fathia Mazumder (11)
Sarah Bonnell School, Stratford

Life

Life is a beautiful story,
Lovely songs can be heard.
Life becomes beautiful,
When sweet memories pass over.
Filled with love, care and happiness,
This all just starts from a void.
You're young until you're not,
You love until you don't,
You try until you can't,
You laugh until you cry,
And everyone must breathe.
You then take the things you love,
Try to love the things you took,
Then take that love you made,
And stick it into someone else's heart.
But here's something important as a part of life:
Success.
Success eludes people,
Who don't try in life,
Success is achieved,
With the right hard work and strife,
Success comes easy,
To those who want it.
Until they never give up.
One thing to remember about life,

Hope.
Hope is the thing with feathers,
That perches in the soul,
And sings the tune without the words,
And never stops at all.

Tasnim Mezhiche (11)
Sarah Bonnell School, Stratford

Bangladesh Independence Day

Echoes of the past ring
In the ears of the living
And remind us of their
Hardships.
Boots march over the souls
Of the lost ones who
Lie on the ground.
Their blood seeps
Into the grass
Nourishing the colonised
Land of the fallen.
Half a century
Goes by and the
Souls of our ancestors
Haunt the land of freedom.
Their grandchildren gather
Rings of flowers all
Over the world to celebrate those
Who gave their lives away.
History has tried to erase them
But will not let go of
Our legacy. We will
Fight and resist against the

Colonisers who tried to steal our
Birthright.
We can never forget them
We can never forget our language
Nor our flag.
That is what we live for
That is what we celebrate
We can never forget Bangladesh.

Rimzim Baser (14)
Sarah Bonnell School, Stratford

Anxiety Is The Only Thing Stopping Me?

The only thing stopping me
Is my anxiety
I feel panicked
When it's inside of me.

Trapped with the feeling of near death
There's an everyday threat, while I'm
Coping with other daily battles
As well as juggling my anxiety
This is how they think I live:
I believe that
Anxiety is the only thing stopping me
It's sad they think that
It's easy to deal with
And it isn't that big of a deal
They really don't know how it feels.

I gathered all my thoughts together
And while very, very focused
I think back to myself
Is my anxiety the only thing stopping me?

Finished? Now read from bottom to top!

Zainab Chowdhury (11)
Sarah Bonnell School, Stratford

Our Future

We are the future.
We took the bullets from our ancestors' shots.
Our future is damaged and fragile.
We are the future.
We have to pay for our ancestors' mistakes.
Our future is stressful and harmful.
We are the future.
We have to take the blame for our ancestors' wrongdoings.
Our future is the scapegoat of all mistakes.
We are the future.
We have to stand up for ourselves if we want anything done.
Our future could be inspiring.
We are the future.
We have to do things the right way and not listen to anyone.
Our future could be rebellious toward tradition.
We are the future.
Children are our future.

Naomi Chima (11)
Sarah Bonnell School, Stratford

Our Burning Desire

We all have burning desires,
Some that may misfire,
But have we ever listened to the Earth's crying choir?

The Earth is burning and that's really fun,
No one believes us because we are young.

Burning,
Our souls are burning with desires of backbiting.
Burning,
Our minds are burning with desires of bad-mouthing.
Burning,
Our hearts are burning with desires of bad intentions.
Burning,
Our mouths are burning with desires of pleading misconceptions.
Burning,
Our hands are burning with desires of showing signs of sad emotions.

Burning, we are all burning.

Saimona Shamim (12)
Sarah Bonnell School, Stratford

To Be Yourself

To be yourself is a choice you can make,
It's what differentiates you and me,
But some people would rather be a fake.

Being yourself, being honest and happy,
That is the goal in many people's lives,
However we still fib and lie,
And that is when problems start to arise,
Problems that lead to friends saying goodbye.

When we do find those friends, good-willed and true,
They will stay for life, through the bad and good,
You should be ready to stay with them too,
Because that is what a true friend will do.

Amanda Jakobsone (13)
Sarah Bonnell School, Stratford

Remedy To An Open Mind

Haiku poetry

Possibilities,
They're here, there and everywhere,
My mind is open.

In challenging times,
I boldly stand mighty tall,
Stay open-minded.

When the storms appear,
Clouding down your self-esteem,
Be open-minded.

When there's hatefulness,
There is also approval,
Be open-minded.

As deprivation
Corrupts the societies,
Stay open-minded.

Grip into finesse,
Blemished by distorted laws,
Stay open-minded.

In the deep stillness,
Where nothing is everything,
I find the answers.

An open mind can
Invite opportunity
That you did not see.

Iram Mazumder (12)
Sarah Bonnell School, Stratford

A Voice

A voice louder than an earthquake,
A voice sharper than a knife,
A voice booming, blooming, boosting,
The confidence of girls around the world,
A voice more powerful than a fist,
Made to change minds rather than fight on the front lines,
Fighting is running rampant,
A voice can make a change,
A voice more powerful than a sword,
A voice belonging to a heart pure and gold,
A voice that will change the world,
Our voice.

Juri Bazan (12)
Sarah Bonnell School, Stratford

Life Isn't Forever

Life is precious, it's not forever
Use it wisely, and be clever
Life is short, don't treat it like trash.

Laugh and smile, you can't buy everything with cash
Life is rare, rarer than a diamond
So don't be rash.

Time goes by like a soldier
As we grow older, we have more things to boulder
A larger chip on our shoulder.

Liyana Begum (12)
Sarah Bonnell School, Stratford

The Shadow

I hear something rustle
Through the pumpkin-orange leaves behind me.
It sounds like a creature,
It doesn't have that many features.
I tread through the forest,
My eyes darting to every corner in sight,
But just then, I feel my heart rate spike.
I feel my skin crawl as the darkest shadows bawl.
Then I find a puddle, it isn't very subtle.
I see my reflection, my, such imperfection.
My face looks dull, like an old rotting skull.
It's bony and white, looking like a skeleton fright.
Then I see it, the figure, I know I won't beat it.
I almost fall into the puddle in fright,
But just then, it is nowhere in sight.
My whole body falls weak, what is it out to seek?
But where? Is it here to scare?
It is just a thought I cannot bare.
I can speak no more, everything is sore.
My breathing is slow, like I've just taken a heavy blow.
I then notice the figure, hiding behind a tree.
When I notice, I know I'm not free.
The darkness creeps upon me like a predator and its prey,
The only thing I can do is cross my heart and pray.

Now, all I can see is darkness,
Amongst it I see...
The shadow.

David Nugent (12)
St Joseph's College, Belfast

Power Of Destruction

The sky is dark, the grass is dry,
Tanks crawl by, and jets speed up like stars moving fast.
Men march by men and war is felt like hell.
People die, children are suffering,
Illness spreads in different countries
Like land without a shield to protect them.
Buildings are destroyed, homes are broken
And they must find a home
To survive the pain of destruction.
But it continues over and over and over every single year
As it is an endless war without rest.
The people who have suffered prayed to God
For the destruction and war to end
And to save their lives so they can see the peace,
The fresh, green grass as soft blades,
Rest and live a happy life,
But they never have them.
Days turn to weeks and weeks turn to months turn to years
And they've given up.
Their lives have been sacrificed for a death sentence
And the leaders of the destruction will never have mercy.
Please save people's lives, stop war, show them peace,
Show them how they feel
And show them that they just wanted a happy life.
Save the people's lives and end the destruction.

Benny Weng (11)
St Joseph's College, Belfast

Stop Ableism

Are we just a disability?
Like a vicious dog off its leash.
Ableism is still happening.
Obvious or invisible, it's still discrimination.
'Disgusting', 'terrifying', 'bad influence' and more.
Stereotype after stereotype after stereotype.
Can't you see we're sick of it?
'Can't do this', 'can't do that'.
How do you know?
Mental or physical, it's still a disability.
All different spectrums.
Masking, isolation, hiding.
It's a daily struggle.
We just want to stop.
We just want acceptance.
Are we only seen as weak?
Are we only seen as a diagnosis?
Why are we not equal?
We demand justice.
We demand to be treated as human.

Grace Duffin (13)
St Joseph's College, Belfast

Shades Of Pink!

Not everything is black and white
Pink bows, blankets and teddy bears
A Barbie doll
Nail polish and gloss
Practising pretty
Household chores
While your brothers play
Short skirts, boyfriends
Eyelashes and make-up
"You're showing too much skin."
"You're being too loud."
"You're hysterical."
"You're asking for it..."
Whistles
Catcalls
Ringing in your ear
A mind of swords
A life in a cage
We can do 'DIY'
We can lift heavy
We can leave the house
We can speak up
Not everything is black and white
We have glorious shades of pink.

Mya McGrattan (14)
St Joseph's College, Belfast

The Devil

Sometimes we die.
We might think about this a lot.
Where will we go... to Heaven?
I think not.
Maybe we go up?
We don't deserve to go up
After all the bad things we have done.
But let's give it a shot.
Come on, let's go down... maybe it's not bad.
It's scorching hot!
What are you waiting for?
Come on, let's go play.
We will meet the haunting ghost, maybe the entities.
But first, let's go down to where we will meet the devil
And where we will fall down to Hell.

Zara Stalker (12)
St Joseph's College, Belfast

The Last Breath

Sweat dripped down my spine like a waterfall,
I heard the birds call,
As I walked home in complete darkness,
Snap. I heard a noise,
I saw a shadow behind me in the light of the lamppost,
Am I being followed? I thought,
I sped up my walk,
Hearing my heartbeat getting louder and faster,
The shadow sped up,
Matching my every step,
Silence...
I stopped,
My heartbeat slowed down,
My head began to spin,
I felt light-headed,
I took a deep breath, trying to calm down,
I looked down at my weak body,
I had been stabbed,
That was my last breath.

Iona Hughes
St Joseph's College, Belfast

Time: More Valuable Than Money

As I spent my free time
Scrolling through the bottomless pit
Called 'social media'
Not anything productive
My plants turned black
I play the radio but I do not care
About the rhymes or the crimes
I was too busy staring at
The tiny screen, 'social media'
Like a tiny encyclopaedia
But why?
Did it make me happy?
Is it worth it
Losing your friends?
Losing your parents, siblings?
Everyone?
All
For
A small screen.

Noel Kunnathparambil (14)
St Joseph's College, Belfast

Shattered

From time to time I find you looking at yourself
The urges filling you whole
The desire to tell yourself about:
How ugly you are
How disappointing you are
How you aren't skinny enough
How you aren't beautiful enough
How you aren't good enough
Looking back at your reflection
With her looking back at you
Wondering the same
Because...
Do you ever wonder if it is time to shatter
The mirror instead of yourself?

Arianna Marcos (13)
St Joseph's College, Belfast

The Power Of Ourselves

Heroes fall, villains rise and pollution is nigh
They who try do not die, but die inside.
We can save them from themselves
And end all of Earth's woes.
But pollution, thy evil will rise once again
Because people don't care for the Earth
And throw it like a ball to the bin.
But we can end all thy troubles
And protect thy beautiful Earth.
The light of the night will guide us through the fight
And help us to show the beauty of our world.

Innes White
St Joseph's College, Belfast

The Front Handspring

I was warm,
And as my hands started to sweat,
My heart was pounding,
Silence commenced,
So many eyes observing me,
I had butterflies,
Nevertheless,
I had to complete my front handspring,
Off I went,
I sprang into the air and flipped,
My mind was racing,
I was about to land,
I stuck the landing,
The crowd started cheering,
It felt as if a weight had been lifted off my shoulders,
I did it.

Anna Mullan
St Joseph's College, Belfast

Our Planet

I am your planet.
I am your life.
You treat me with respect or you won't stay alive,
The Earth will die.
Look after me and help my lungs to breathe
By being eco-warriors and looking after trees.
This is your planet. It's our space.
We will look after it,
Or it will fade away.
Recycle your rubbish,
Change your habits
To live a longer and better life.

Filip Niedziolka (13)
St Joseph's College, Belfast

My Dog Rosie

She is small and fierce
With tiny paws.
She has small sharp teeth
In her jaws.

She's fluffy and cute and
Doesn't listen at all.
She'd run off and would never come back
Even if you tried to call.

She loves to walk slow or fast
She keeps stopping to smell as
She knows the walk won't last.

When she was small she chewed up a shoe
Now I don't know what we'd do without you.
Rosie.

Aaron McKenna (12)
St Joseph's College, Belfast

The War Evacuee

Violence and explosions
Crumbling and cracking the earth
All portrayed with dire emotions.
Standing atop the lifeless hill
Devoid of nature
Accepting torture
Watching the skies burning
A bright red glow illuminating the land.
The screech of thrusters splitting
The sky. Bursting eardrums and
Corroding memory... with ferocious
Fear.

Tom Magee (14)
St Joseph's College, Belfast

Fairies

My heart believes in things my eyes can't see,
To be able to be a tiny little fairy,
Prancing through the summer breeze,
I would fly into my hollowed-out tree,
Followed by a nice, winter-long sleep,
Oh, to be a fairy, I wish and pray,
Not yet, but maybe one day.

Lauren McCafferty (12)
St Joseph's College, Belfast

Silly Sausages

Silly sausages, oh how tasty,
You can have them in a pastry,
That is called a sausage roll,
The moment I tasted the beautiful thing, it changed my soul,
Sausage rolls are very popular, so,
I cannot wait, I better go!

Sarah Jane McCrumlish
St Joseph's College, Belfast

Fish

If a genie gave me one wish,
It would be to get a cute fish.
Whether it be a goldfish, a clownfish or a blobfish,
Or it be blue, purple or orange,
Or it be stripy, spotty,
Big or small,
I would want them all!

Rachel Nelson
St Joseph's College, Belfast

Cost Of Living

Prices up and up and up.
Stock running out and out.
The poor are struggling.
The rich are feeling a big difference.
What is going on?
Fifteen pence to twenty-five pence.
Fifty pence to seventy pence.
The price rise is increasing.
Where are the oil, gas and petrol going?
Why is it running out?
Families are struggling.
Parents under pressure to feed their loved ones.
Wishing this can lead to something good!
What is going on?

Ciara Cunningham (12)
St Louis Grammar School, Kilkeel

Our World

Let's talk about our future
It's going to be quite the lecture
People are littering our great sea
It's not a nice thing to see
We need to help Ukraine
To stop Russia's reign
Our world is heating up
And Antarctica is turning to slush
Our ice caps are melting
Our oceans are rising
Stop a plastic world
Create a clean reality
Cure the virus
Fund the ones in need
So please
Put our Earth
At ease.

Jack Doran (11)
St Louis Grammar School, Kilkeel

Climate Change

We watch the Earth slowly die
And sometimes we just close our eyes.
Just imagine a nice, clean park
And how it could improve someone's walk.
Everyone can help in a way,
You could do something that takes a little of your time.
So many animals have been extinct
Due to climate change and deforestation.
We need to stop killing our Earth
And fight for what's right!

Miya Russell (11)
St Louis Grammar School, Kilkeel

Identity

Your identity is a big part of your life.
It makes you, you.
Trying to be like others.
Isn't what you're supposed to do.
So just be you.

Emilia Rose Gren (12)
St Louis Grammar School, Kilkeel

Who'll Join Me To Fight?

Who will join me to fight to end animal cruelty?
To end the crying homeless animals
That are beaten into tiny cages?
Who'll help me save all the traumatised animals?
Would you save a brutally injured animal
Like how you would save a starving homeless child?

Who won't put up with climate change?
The horrific earthquakes, the terrible tsunamis.
Who wants an end to the vicious wildfires
That kill and suffocate?

Who's ready for LGBTQ+ rights?
An end to hate in showing differences.
Who will fight for what's right?

Who wants to end black hate?
Who won't put up with racism
And stick up for those
Who are getting hurt for being different?
The hate for people that are no different from us,
That are not doing anything wrong
And being punished for being different?

Jessica Housley (13)
Stretford High School, Stretford

The Reality Of War

Round one,
There were a lot of cons.
It was not what I was told,
The thing was, it was just too cold.
I had to fight,
So I could get a bite.
Victory, it's what I needed,
I hoped I could still get my deed.

Round two,
"What are they up to?"
"I don't know, but the sky ain't blue."
I could hear a boom,
It made my ears ring,
My mate responded saying, "Kaboom."

Round three,
I had to watch by a tree.
I was paralysed in fear,
Even though I couldn't hear.
Fear,
It was all I could think,
As the sky went pink.
I could see the take come in,
And blast my surroundings.

Round four,
The rain began to pour.
This was the point when the gas came,
And me? Man I was bummed.
The war was not over, never to be,
Though for now, we just had to see...
The death toll was in the millions,
Though we still needed some resilience.

Round five,
The war wasn't kind.
Luckily for us,
We had gotten a bus.
A bus back home.
I was excited about what was to come,
And I just hoped that the house wasn't gone.

Matthew Cooke (12)
Stretford High School, Stretford

The Life Of A Soldier

The life of a soldier,
Oh so weary,
The life of a soldier,
Bleak and dreary.

Bombs, gunshots, that's all we hear,
No smell of victory,
Not anywhere near,
A whole lot of contradictory,
Do you feel sympathy?
The life of a soldier,
The perfect epitome.

A hero they said I would be,
Unquestionably I disagree,
Lies on top of lies, I see,
The complete opposite, I plea.

Nevertheless, I do it for my country,
For who will save us?
No hero in a cape,
Just me and my comrades,
No choice or way to escape.

The life of a soldier,
Oh so weary,
The life of a soldier,
Bleak and dreary.

To suffer we did not choose,
Yet we have nothing to lose,
Non-combatants with different views,
Having to pick and choose,
This is my side of the story,
All the untold truths.

Izah Maroof (13)
Stretford High School, Stretford

I'll Make It Out Alive

There's mud on the ground
People with a frown
They all mask their sadness
And desire to die
With a sweet and welcoming smile
What a bittersweet lie
The poor diet
My trench feet
We eat, sleep and fight
"But we will be alright..."
Says the man standing amongst corpses
We walk away as if we never saw it
Rats that are the same size as cats
Nothing makes it worse
Than the space, it's so cramped
Ten days in this mess
With hardly any rest
"I'll make it out alive!"
I say to the dead
As a bomb in the sky
Blows up my sixteen-year-old head.

Inha Cho (13)
Stretford High School, Stretford

My Country

The pages have flipped, the tables have turned
My life is no longer as I yearned
My family, so far away
Hoping that they will see me one day
We need to unite
To see the light
And make sure the country's future is bright.

They are the tyrants
Through all their violence
But we won't be silenced
They might try to kill me
For love is what they can't see.

Looking around
Dead corpses lying around
Gas flooding us like a tide
Where shall we go? Where shall we hide?
What will happen if I go?
Who will end this gruesome show?

Khadijah Timol (12)
Stretford High School, Stretford

War

The ground shakes uncontrollably beneath my feet,
That once stood nice and neat,
But now I'm here in a brutal place,
A place where there's anything but peace,
A place where there's no life,
A place where you have to carry a knife.

Boom! The sound of trauma in the distance,
The sound of cries,
The sound of lies,
The sound of bombs taking people's homes,
The sounds you will never forget.

Guns, explosions, death,
Oh! Give me back my health.

Eshal Nasir (13)
Stretford High School, Stretford

Despair

Skies as black as the hearts of the dead,
Men bony; crippled and unfed,
Fires roar loud and proud,
Diseases spread as fast as sound,
Soldiers tearing left and right,
"But we are strong so we shall fight."

Birds fleeing; chopped and bruised,
The Navy are on a sorrowful cruise,
Sunlight empty in the shadow of the clouds,
The men are now too sick and shroud,
"If we can't seek the blessings of light,"
"Why shall we raise our guns and fight?"

Stephanie Nyavi (12)
Stretford High School, Stretford

Ashes

The sound of gunshots,
Makes our heads ache.
The sight of dead bodies,
Makes our hearts ache.
Do we deserve this pain?

Even the word 'war' sounds insane.
In here it's so dirty and cold,
I'm going to be here till I'm old.

The feeling of fear rules our hearts
As we pray in agony and despair.

The fear of never going back disrupts our sleep.
Come on,
Let's win this!
Or our whole country will turn into
Ashes!

Eshal Chowdhary (13)
Stretford High School, Stretford

Night, Fear, War

The night. The time when I feel a sense of fright.
The night. The time when I have the instinct to fight.
The night. The time when I help make things right.
The night. The time when I have to use all my might.

Fear. The feeling that I am unaware of what's near.
Fear. A feeling of pounding in my ear.
Fear. A feeling that my life is out of control and I cannot steer.

War. Where violence is at its core.
War. Where you get closer to death's door.

Kuljeet Singh (13)
Stretford High School, Stretford

War

Bombs, guns, tanks,
I am tired of this,
Each and every day,
We go out hunting for our enemies,
But come back with solemn faces,
As no enemy has been caught,
Oh how I wish this war stopped,
It was all a lie,
A big lie,
I'm telling you,
Don't let anyone fool you,
Don't let your life get ruined,
Like mine has,
All I need is my family,
But our general will not stop fighting,
And we won't stop fighting for him.

Tayyaba Wahid (12)
Stretford High School, Stretford

World War

Boom. The sound of bombs in the distance,
Blood dripping from my face.
Boom. Explosions start again,
We all grab a gun and start to pick up the pace.

The ground rumbles under my feet,
As people get shot repetitively,
The ones that stood nice and neat,
But are no longer here,
Guns, explosions, death,
My heart racing in my head,
Walking through these small, cramped trenches,
Oh, Lord! Please bring back my health.

Umaimah Bhana (12)
Stretford High School, Stretford

Who's For The Earth?

Who's for the Earth, the big gleaming giant?
Who will save her from crumbling like a big paper ball?
Who'll sacrifice their lives and dreams to cool down the planet
To stop her from drowning in the heat?
And who will rewind what we have done?
Why lay at home awaiting the planet's doom
Instead of trying to find the solution we all need?
Who will fight this problem and cool down our big blue planet?

Marley Barrett (12)
Stretford High School, Stretford

The Real War

I aim high, no stopping
I see bodies dropping
This life ain't funny
Why did I see three dead bodies?
Not one of them had blood that was runny
My friends are dead
I think it is okay
I know this is a ruthless game
Finance is zero
Kills are 101
Most kills in the game, I'm one of one.

Salman Alam (13)
Stretford High School, Stretford

Fearing

Explosions constantly bombard around me
Threats are always constant
When will it stop?
Is it a dream?

Who knows?
Sticking up your heads above the trench
Is a horrible way to death's door.

Muhammed Ali (13)
Stretford High School, Stretford

The Moon And The Stars

Shall we look at the moon and the stars?
Constellations trace the sky like scars
Showing tales of broken hearts
The moon watches over, an eye in the sky
It glares at us all, as it wades by
A ball of rock, yet it controls all the tides
A powerful being, so mysterious to question why
Why does it simply float by?
The stars have names they call themselves by
Sirius, Bellatrix, Mira, Lupi
Burning up
Do you think they cry?

Isla Pullin
Tarleton Academy, Tarleton

A New World

A new start,
Something we all want,
Change what we did wrong,
And make the things that were right better,
But that isn't impossible.

People make unchangeable decisions every day,
From the little things about what you want to eat,
To the big ones like bombs or other dreadful things,
The big ones nearly all lead to the same things,
People getting hurt.

Humanity is the best thing,
New inventions,
Life-saving medicines,
All intend to make our lives easier,
But when that one person makes that unchangeable decision,
It hurts everyone.

Not just the people affected physically,
But those who can't bear the reality,
Of this happening in modern-day society,
Those people who are affected mentally as well.

We can't let this happen,
All the groups and laws we have,
It shouldn't,
Can't be possible.

Then you look at the problem of poverty,
Everyone has seen it,
Every week a new charity on the TV,
Every week saying the same thing,
People don't have enough to survive.

They don't have enough money to even buy breakfast,
And that they can only drink dirty water,
Just like people getting hurt,
It shouldn't be allowed to happen.

All those people living their luxurious lives,
All while people struggle to even get through the day,
We need to help them,
As much as we can,
Even though we can't give everything,
The little things count,
If we make that decision to help, a lot of people will benefit.

Then we move to the single biggest problem facing us,
The one that won't only affect our generation,
But the next,
And the next,
Climate change,

Global warming,
Whatever you call it,
It doesn't change the severity of the situation.

It's silly,
Something that we are already seeing the effects of,
But yet we still drive around, oblivious to the bigger picture,
Every day it gets worse,
But it's not just our fault,
The bigger powers need to do something,
To make electric cars more accessible.

After all, we end up at the same thing,
A new start.

Just imagine how different the world would be if we restarted,
Kept our knowledge,
All the big conflicts in history wouldn't happen.

There is one thing to improve the world,
Think before we do,
Then everything will become better.

So a new start means a new world,
No,
We don't need it,
Because if we want a new world,
We make it.

Joseph Vose (13)
Tarleton Academy, Tarleton

Young Writers
Est. 1991

Young Writers Information

We hope you have enjoyed reading this book – and that you will continue to in the coming years.

If you're the parent or family member of an enthusiastic poet or story writer, do visit our website **www.youngwriters.co.uk/subscribe** and sign up to receive news, competitions, writing challenges and tips, activities and much, much more! There's lots to keep budding writers motivated!

If you would like to order further copies of this book, or any of our other titles, then please give us a call or order via your online account.

Young Writers
Remus House
Coltsfoot Drive
Peterborough
PE2 9BF
(01733) 890066
info@youngwriters.co.uk

Join in the conversation!
Tips, news, giveaways and much more!

YoungWritersUK   YoungWritersCW   youngwriterscw